TWENTY DATES LATER

A Romantic Comedy About Love, Faith, and Laughably Bad Dates

CHARLIE H. CAMPBELL

This is a work of fiction. Names, characters, organizations, places, events, images of people, and incidents are either products of the author's imagination or are used fictitiously. Descriptions of and references to events in the Bible are factual.

TWENTY DATES LATER:
A Romantic Comedy About Love, Faith, and Laughably Bad Dates

Copyright © 2025 by Charles H. Campbell.
Published by Always Be Ready
P. O. Box 130342, Carlsbad CA 92013
Email: abr@alwaysbeready.com

Additional copies of this book can be found at **AlwaysBeReady.com**

ISBN: Paperback: 9798313828626

Cover design and interior layout by the author.
Printed in the United States of America.

TWENTY DATES LATER

*A Romantic Comedy About Love, Faith,
and Laughably Bad Dates*

CHARLIE H. CAMPBELL

Warning:
Reading this book may cause uncontrollable
laughter, secondhand embarrassment, and the
awkward experience of cackling in public
with no way to explain why.

Contents

Prologue

The 20-Date Disaster Challenge

I'm Berkely Monroe, and I've officially concluded that dating as a Christian woman is like walking through a minefield in stilettos. Blindfolded. While someone plays the theme song from *Jaws*.

You think you're about to meet a great guy—someone who loves Jesus, has a solid job, and can hold a conversation without quoting a podcast verbatim. But then you sit down, and he hits you with:

- "I don't believe in washing my jeans."

- "I think women aren't as funny as men, but you seem cool though."
- "I think the government controls the weather. But don't worry, I have a plan."

And suddenly, you're gripping your fork like a weapon, contemplating your escape route.

For the past *several* years, I had given Christian dating apps, church groups, set-ups, and random Whole Foods encounters everything I had to give. And for what?

Pam.

Not my date's name—*his mother's.*

I knew something was off when we walked into the restaurant and he casually said, *"Oh, Mom's already here."*

I blinked. "I'm sorry—what?"

He smiled like this was completely normal. "Yeah, I just thought it'd be great if you two met right away."

I froze. "You . . . *brought your mom*?"

"She insisted!" He laughed, completely unbothered. "She even picked the restaurant!"

Lord, give me strength.

I followed him to the table, where a woman in a pastel cardigan was already seated, waving enthusiastically.

"You must be Berkely!" she gushed. "I'm *Pam!*"

Of course she was.

I shook her hand, still too stunned to react. My date—who I had spoken to *exactly twice* before tonight—pulled out a chair for me, then one for his mother, and then one for himself.

Pam smiled warmly. "I'm so happy to finally meet you."

Finally?

"I told her all about you," my date said, nudging my arm.

I turned to stare at him. "Have you?"

"Oh yes!" Pam beamed. "He said you could be *the one!*"

I choked on my own spit.

Pam reached across the table and patted my hand. "Don't worry, sweetheart. I'm an excellent judge of character. And I already have a good feeling about you."

I stared at her, then at my date, then at the door—the door that suddenly seemed *very* far away.

Things unraveled quickly from there:

- Pam did *all* the talking. I was barely halfway through my salad before I knew her thoughts on politics, organic groceries, and *which* shade of ivory I should consider for my future wedding dress.
- My date was *thrilled* about all of it. "See? She *loves* you."
- Pam casually mentioned that *she* would be joining us on our honeymoon.

I did not ask for clarification. I did not want clarification.

By the time the check arrived, I had aged three years.

Pam hugged me tightly. "We'll talk *soon,* dear."

I did not respond.

And that was it. That was the moment I knew. I had hit rock bottom.

Which is how I ended up on my couch later that night, dramatically announcing my resignation from dating to my roommate, Claire.

She was half-listening, flipping through a magazine as I paced the living room. "I'm done, Claire. That was my last date. I am officially quitting."

"No, you're not."

"I am."

"You are not."

"I am."

Claire smirked. "Fine. But I was reading an article recently that said a lot of singles give up on dating too soon, and if they'd just commit to twenty more first dates, they'd have a 95% chance of meeting their spouse."

I stopped pacing. "Claire."

She leaned forward, eyes sparkling with mischief. "No, listen. *Twenty* first dates. That's all I ask."

I crossed my arms. "Claire. I would rather let

Pam plan my wedding *and* pick my honeymoon destination."

Claire gasped. "You take that back."

I shook my head. "Nope. This is my hard line."

She clapped her hands. "Twenty dates. That's all I ask."

I groaned and flopped onto the couch. "I hate everything."

Claire patted my knee. "No, you don't. You love me. And in twenty dates, you're gonna love your husband too."

I let my head loll to the side. "If I survive."

Claire beamed. "That's the spirit!"

And just like that, my fate was sealed.

Twenty dates.

Lord, help me.

Date 1

There were many things I expected from tonight's first date.

Good conversation? Sure.

A decent meal? Hopefully.

A romantic connection that finally justified all my time on dating apps? *Maybe.*

You know what I did *not* expect?

Lice.

I was mid-sentence when I saw it.

Something wiggling in his hair.

I froze.

". . . Berkely?"

My date, Chad—*who I had been talking to for a full twenty minutes*—tilted his head, blinking at me.

I stared.

Then, very slowly, I said,

"There's something . . . moving."

Chad blinked. "Moving?"

I nodded. "In your hair."

Chad frowned. Then, without warning, he scratched his head.

Hard.

Like a man who has been deeply suffering in silence.

And that's when I realized—

Oh my gosh.

This man.

This actual, grown adult man.

Had lice.

It got worse.

Because instead of being horrified, embarrassed, or even mildly concerned, Chad shrugged.

"Oh yeah," he said casually. "I've been dealing with that for a while."

I choked.

"A while?"

He nodded. "Yeah. My nephew had it a few months ago, and I guess I caught it."

I stared at him in pure, unfiltered horror.

"You . . . *guess?*"

Chad took a very casual sip of his water. "Yeah, it comes and goes."

IT. COMES. AND. GOES.

Like it was seasonal allergies or something.

Like it wasn't a full-blown parasite infestation.

I sat there, paralyzed, my scalp already itching in sympathy.

And then, because I truly had nothing left to lose, I set down my fork, looked Chad right in the eye, and said,

"I have to go."

Five minutes later, I was driving home, screaming internally.

I had burned my dating outfit in my mind.

I had ordered overnight lice shampoo, just in case.

And I had texted Claire with a simple, straightforward message:

Berkely: I'm done.

Claire: With what?

Berkely: Dating. Men. Hope. Life.

Claire: Wow. Date went that well, huh?

Berkely: Claire. He had LICE.

Claire: OH MY GOSH.

Claire: Like confirmed, textbook, real-life lice??

Berkely: It comes and goes, Claire.

Claire: BERKELY, NO.

The next night, Claire was waiting for me when I got home.

The moment I opened the door, she tossed me a bottle of lice shampoo.

I caught it midair. "Wow. No hello?"

She flopped onto the couch, grinning. "You survived."

I sighed, tossing my bag onto the counter. "Barely."

Claire pulled out her phone. "I already drafted your next profile."

I groaned. "Claire—"

"You're committed, Berk. Twenty first dates. That's the deal."

I sank into the couch and covered my face. "Claire, I'm still emotionally recovering."

She ignored me. "Alright, so I put your bio as: 'Love Jesus, sarcasm, and tacos. Looking for someone who won't give me lice.'"

I sat up. "You didn't."

She turned her phone around.

She absolutely did.

I groaned. "You are the actual worst."

Claire just beamed. "Date Two is tomorrow. Let me know if I need to fake an emergency."

Date 2

I knew the night had taken a turn when my date pulled a coupon out of his wallet and proudly slapped it on the table.

"There it is," Greg announced, grinning. "Half off appetizers. You're welcome."

I stared at the crumpled, slightly greasy coupon. Then up at Greg, who looked entirely too pleased with himself.

I sighed.

One down.

Nineteen to go.

Greg leaned back in his chair, arms crossed

like he'd just done me some grand romantic favor.

"Wow," I said. "You really went all out."

He nodded. "I almost used it last week, but I figured I'd save it for someone special."

This. This was my life.

The server came by, and Greg insisted on ordering for me. "She'll have the buffalo wings, and I'll take the spinach dip." He winked at me. "Ladies love buffalo wings."

"Not this lady," I said.

Greg frowned. "Oh. Well, too late."

I opened my mouth to protest, but the server was already gone. Greg shrugged. "You'll love 'em. Trust me."

I did not, in fact, love them.

And that was before he asked me to *chip in* on the half-off appetizers.

"Sorry," I said, staring at him, unsure if I'd heard correctly.

"For the wings," Greg said, pulling out his phone and opening a payment app. "Just Venmo me like, six bucks. Unless you wanna leave the tip?"

I exhaled slowly. "Greg."

"Yeah?"

"I'm not Venmo-ing you six dollars for the half-off appetizer that you ordered *for me.*"

His face scrunched in genuine confusion. "Oh. Huh." He tapped his fingers on the table, considering. "Okay, what if I cover the wings, and you just get the tip?"

My soul left my body.

The date, somehow, continued. Over dinner, Greg explained his entire investment strategy (spoiler: it involved crypto and flipping rare Pokémon cards), showed me a spreadsheet of his ex-girlfriends (ranked *by compatibility*, no less), and finished the meal by informing me that, quote, *girls don't actually like flowers as much as they pretend to.*

I downed the last of my water and stood. "Well, this has been . . . something."

Greg grinned. "Awesome?"

I grabbed my purse. "Sure."

Outside, I took a deep breath of freedom.

Then another, just for good measure.

Claire was so going to hear about this.

At home, I flopped onto my couch and texted her.

Berkely: Two down.

Claire: LOL. What happened??

Berkely: Let's just say my appetizer was half-off, and so was my dignity.

Claire sent a laughing emoji.

Berkely: Eighteen more, and then I'm done.

Her response came fast.

Claire: That's the spirit!

I tossed my phone onto the couch and closed my eyes.

Eighteen more.

Then I was done.

For good.

Date 3

When Claire told me she had the perfect guy for Date Three, I should have known better.
I really should have.

I was picturing a normal walk at the park. A nice, low-pressure way to get to know someone without the distractions of a loud restaurant or Claire live-texting me from across the room.

I was not picturing this.

"His name's Ringo," Troy said, adjusting the tiny harness on his ferret.

I blinked. "I'm sorry . . . what?"

Troy beamed. "Ringo! He's my little dude."

I looked down at the literal ferret standing at my feet. A long, slinky creature wearing a harness and leash, blinking up at me like he, too, was judging my life choices.

We stood in an open field at the park, birds chirping, the sun shining, and Troy acting completely normal as if we weren't about to take a romantic sunset stroll with a semi-domesticated weasel.

I pasted on a polite smile. "So, um . . . how long have you had him?"

"Oh, years," Troy said, giving Ringo an affectionate pat. "I don't go anywhere without him."

I swallowed. "Anywhere?"

"Yup. He's my emotional support animal."

Lord, give me strength.

I nodded slowly, trying to process. "Right. So, like . . . do you take him places? Restaurants?"

Troy chuckled. "Oh, absolutely. People love him. He just chills in my hoodie."

I blinked. "In your . . ."

Before I could finish, Troy gave a little whistle and patted his chest. The ferret—who had been sniffing around near his feet—perked up, then launched itself up his leg like a tiny, unhinged acrobat. It scrambled up his torso, disappeared into the front pocket of his oversized hoodie, and settled in like it was paying rent.

I clutched my drink. "Oh. My. Gosh."

Troy grinned, patting the lump now moving under his hoodie. "See? He loves it in there. Keeps me warm in the winter."

I sucked in a sharp breath, watching in horror as the lump shifted and repositioned like a tiny, living horror movie. "You just . . . let him do that?"

Troy laughed. "Yeah! He's basically my little sidekick."

I stared at the hoodie like it might start moving on its own. I was on a date with a man who had a built-in, live-action chestburster scene, and I didn't know how to escape.

Troy grinned.

Before I could respond, Ringo poked his tiny head out of the hoodie's front pocket.

I choked. "TROY."

Troy laughed. "He likes it in there! Keeps him warm."

I put a hand to my forehead. "Okay, but— what if you get too hot? Or need to take off your hoodie?"

Troy frowned like this had never once occurred to him. "Huh." He looked down at Ringo. "You okay with that, bud?"

The ferret licked his own eyeball.

That was it. I was done.

I FaceTimed Claire as soon as I got home.

She answered on the first ring. "Well?"

I exhaled dramatically. "Claire. The man had a ferret in his hoodie."

Claire screamed.

"I went on a romantic walk with a rodent on a leash."

Claire wheezed, clutching her stomach. "I LOVE THIS FOR YOU."

"Claire," I deadpanned. "His name was Ringo."

She lost it.

I sighed. "Seventeen more, Claire. Just seventeen more."

Date 4

Some people make questionable life choices.

Some people broadcast those questionable life choices over dinner.

And some people—like Date Four—choose violence.

His name was Ryan. He was cute, polite, and seemed normal. I actually started to relax.

Until the food arrived.

And I made the mistake of complimenting his jacket.

"Thanks," Ryan said, picking up his fork. "I've had it for years."

I smiled. "Nice! Vintage?"

He chuckled. "Sort of. It's actually never been washed."

I froze. "I'm sorry?"

"Oh yeah." Ryan nodded casually. "I don't wash my jackets. Or my jeans."

I nearly dropped my fork.

". . . You don't?"

"Nah." He waved a hand. "They say you don't need to. Washing them messes with the fibers."

I stared. "Who . . . who is 'they'?"

He shrugged. "You know. The experts."

I had so many follow-up questions.

What experts.

What fibers.

WHAT DO YOU MEAN, 'NEVER BEEN WASHED'??

I took a sip of water, trying to breathe through the horror.

He noticed my expression and laughed. "Oh, don't worry, I clean them in other ways."

I brightened. "Oh! Like dry cleaning?"

Ryan shook his head. "Nah, nah. Freezing them."

I blinked. "I . . . I'm sorry, what now?"

"Freezing!" he said cheerfully. "You just put them in the freezer overnight. Kills bacteria."

I set down my fork.

Ryan kept going, totally unfazed. "It's actually better for the fabric."

I stared at my plate, doing mental gymnastics.

". . . So you just . . . put your dirty clothes in with your food?"

"Oh, I double-bag them," he assured me. "Usually."

Usually.

I swallowed hard. "Ryan. When was the last time your jeans were actually washed?"

He frowned, considering. "Hmm. Good question. At least five years?"

Five.

Years.

I closed my eyes. "Lord, be near."

"BERKELY."

I had barely answered the call when Claire screamed.

I sighed. "Claire. I have suffered."

Claire was already crying. "YOU DATED A MAN WHO FREEZES HIS CLOTHES?"

I nodded solemnly. "I walked through the valley of shadow and death."

Claire wiped her eyes. "Was he—oh my gosh—was he wearing dirty jeans?"

I exhaled. "Claire. They were stiff."

She lost it.

I rubbed my temples. "Sixteen more, Claire. Just sixteen more."

Date 5

By Date Five, I had reached a dangerous level of emotional detachment.

At this point, I wasn't even hoping for romance—I was just bracing for whatever fresh nonsense was about to unfold.

Which is why, when I walked into the restaurant and spotted my date leaning back in the booth, grinning like he owned the place, I knew.

I just knew.

This was going to be a disaster.

And reader? I was right.

The moment I stepped inside, I saw him.

Brandon. Mid-thirties, slightly-too-tight polo shirt, hair gelled to perfection. He was sprawled across the booth like it was his throne, wearing a smirk that immediately activated my fight-or-flight response.

As soon as I sat down, he hit me with a full set of veneers and a "Hey there, sweetheart."

Sweetheart. Strike one.

"Hey," I said, scooting into my seat. "So, how's your day been?"

He smirked. "Better now that you're here."

Strike two.

I gave a polite, noncommittal laugh and prayed for a painless evening. The server came by, and Brandon ordered a steak—medium rare—then turned to me.

"You like salad, right?"

I blinked. "Excuse me?"

"You'll love the garden salad here. Super fresh." He nodded at the server. "She'll take that."

I stared. "Oh. Will I?"

He winked. "Gotta keep that figure in check."

Strike three.

The server hesitated, as if she, too, was considering throwing a drink in his face. I forced a tight smile. "Actually, I'll have the burger. Extra fries."

Brandon's eyebrow twitched, like I'd just announced my allegiance to the dark side. But I didn't care. The man had literally menu-shamed me on a first date.

As the night dragged on, Brandon made sure to hit every red flag possible.

Talked about himself for forty-five straight minutes.

Called his ex-girlfriend 'crazy' (without any further details).

Casually mentioned that 'women aren't as funny as men' but followed up with, "I mean, you seem cool, though."

By the time dessert rolled around, I was mentally checked out, staring at my fries like they were my last thread of sanity.

Then the server approached and asked if we'd like to see the menu.

Before I could even respond, Brandon

grinned and slapped the table.

"Actually, it's her birthday!"

My head snapped toward him. "Excuse me?"

Brandon just winked. "Gotta play it cool, babe." Then he turned back to the server, lowering his voice like we were accomplices in some great heist. "You guys do a free dessert for birthdays, right?"

The server's face lit up. "Of course! Let me grab the whole team."

I sat there, stunned, as the realization hit me like a slow-motion car crash.

This was not the first time he had done this.

This man—this fully grown adult man—had a system for scamming restaurants out of free desserts.

And then.

The servers arrived.

A full team, clapping and singing.

"HAAAAPPY BIRTHDAY TO YOUUUU—"

I sat frozen, soul crushed under the weight of my existence, as the entire restaurant turned to watch me suffer.

Brandon leaned back in his seat, beaming like a proud con artist.

They finished the song, set down the dessert, and I slowly stood up.

Brandon blinked up at me. "Where are you going?"

I grabbed my purse, smiled sweetly, and patted his shoulder.

"Enjoy your free birthday dessert, Brandon."

And with that, I walked out.

I made it to the parking lot before I heard him calling after me:

"Wait—so you don't want any??"

Later That Night . . .

I FaceTimed Claire, collapsing onto my couch in frustration. "Five dates, Claire. Five. And we've already had a coupon guy, a ferret guy, a no-laundry guy, and whatever that was."

Claire cackled. "You're doing the Lord's work. I've never been more entertained."

"I'm glad someone is enjoying my suffering." I

sighed. "Fifteen more."

She hummed in thought, then paused. "Hey, whatever happened to Keagan? He was always around."

I made a face. "Keagan? No. That was forever ago."

Claire just smirked. "Mm-hmm."

I rolled my eyes. "Focus, Claire. We still have fifteen disasters to go."

And with that, I threw my phone onto the couch and closed my eyes.

Fifteen more.

Then I was done.

For good.

Date 6

There's emotional vulnerability on a first date.

And then there's having a full-on breakdown in the middle of Olive Garden.

Jake was cute. He was nice. He was clearly not over his ex.

I should have seen the signs earlier.

First five minutes? He casually mentioned an ex.

Ten minutes in? He brought her up again.

Fifteen minutes in? I was fully on the ride and could not escape.

"She just . . . she meant so much to me, you know?"

I nodded slowly. "Right. And when did you

two break up?"

Jake stared at his breadstick like it had personally betrayed him.

"Last week."

I choked. "I'm sorry—WHAT."

He nodded, eyes watering. "Yeah. It's been a journey."

I took the biggest sip of water of my life.

Jake sniffled.

"I just . . ." His voice wobbled. "I still see her in my dreams."

I put a hand to my forehead.

He wiped his eyes. "So what about you? What's your worst breakup?"

I smiled politely. "This one."

Post-Date Summary:
- Date #6 → A free therapy session.
- Me? Emotionally drained.
- Jake? Still crying.
- Claire? Laughing forever.

Fourteen more. Then I was done.

Date 7

By Date Seven, I was convinced that God was either testing my patience or personally orchestrating these dates to build my character.

Either way, I had some follow-up questions.

Date Six had been a disaster of its own, one I had already relived in horrifying detail. But Date Seven? That was a different breed of catastrophe.

I should have known something was off when he refused to sit near the windows..

"Too risky," he muttered, glancing around.

I blinked. "I'm sorry . . . too risky for what?"

He leaned forward, voice low.

"You really think they don't have eyes everywhere?"

I froze mid-menu scan.

". . . I'm sorry, what?"

He exhaled sharply. "I just wasn't expecting you to be one of *them*."

I stared.

One of who.

His name was Mitch. He was 30, had intense eye contact, and wore a T-shirt that said WAKE UP SHEEPLE. He had refused to text me on any messaging app because *"the Feds are tracking emojis."* And within three minutes of sitting down, he had already asked:

- "Do you honestly believe the moon landing happened?"
- "Ever felt like a bird was watching you?"
- "Do you think this menu is bugged?"

I sent Claire a frantic text under the table.
Me: CLAIRE.

Claire: Oh no. What now?

Me: HE JUST IMPLIED THAT BIRDS ARE GOVERNMENT DRONES.

Claire: Oh, absolutely not.

Me: HE'S LOOKING AT ME LIKE I MIGHT BE A FED.

Claire: I cannot stress this enough: GET OUT.

The waitress arrived, and Mitch stared at her nametag like he was trying to decode it.

"I'll take the grilled chicken," I said quickly.

Mitch scoffed.

"Do you know what's in that?"

I paused.

". . . Chicken?"

He shook his head gravely.

"No. Chemicals. Tracking agents. The government puts it in mass-produced poultry to weaken our brainwaves."

I blinked slowly.

The waitress froze.

Mitch nodded, satisfied. "I'll have the burger. No bun. No lettuce. No onions. No pickles."

The waitress hesitated. "So . . . just the patty?"

Mitch tapped his temple. "Can't be too careful."

She stared. Then turned to me. "And to drink?"

I opened my mouth.

Mitch cut me off.

"She'll have water, no ice."

I turned to gape at him.

Mitch shook his head. "You don't want to know what's in fluoridated tap water."

I turned back to the waitress.

"Make it a Diet Coke."

Mitch looked personally betrayed.

I pulled out my phone and started texting Claire again.

Me: CLAIRE.

Claire: What.

Me: HE JUST SAID 5G GIVES US CAVITIES.

Claire: LEAVE.

Me: HE THINKS THE AIRPORT TSA SCANNERS STEAL YOUR DNA.

Claire: BERKELY.
Me: I THINK HE'S TRYING TO FIGURE
OUT IF I'M A REPTILE.
Claire: RUN.

Mitch sighed.

"You probably think I sound crazy."

I laughed nervously. "You could say that."

He leaned forward.

"So . . . be honest. Have you ever felt like you were being *watched*?"

I frowned. "You mean, like . . . right now?"

"No, no," he whispered. "Like, *in your every-day life?* Ever get a feeling like there's something just out of sight, tracking your every move?"

I squinted. "You mean . . . God?"

Mitch's eye twitched.

"Okay," he said slowly, "but *besides* Him."

I stared at him.

"Are we back to the birds?"

Mitch tapped his nose meaningfully.

By the time the check arrived, I had learned:

- The Pentagon has a weather-controlling machine.
- Grocery store barcodes track "how obedient you are."
- His uncle knows a guy who saw Bigfoot "on accident."

As I reached for my purse, Mitch held up a hand.

"I got this," he said smoothly.

I blinked. "Oh. Thanks."

He smirked. "No problem. It's not my money anyway."

I paused mid-reach.

". . . I'm sorry, what?"

Mitch grinned.

"I only pay with cash. The second you put your card down, they got you."

I stared so hard my vision blurred.

"Who is . . . *they?*"

He tapped his temple again.

"You'll see."

And that was the last time I let a guy hit me with a conspiracy-laced monologue before the appetizer arrived.

Date #7 – A psychological thriller disguised as a dinner.

Me? Exhausted.

Mitch? Probably living off the grid in a bunker somewhere.

(*Spoiler: I am losing my will to continue this experiment.*)

That night, I curled up on the couch, phone in hand, ready for my daily post-date debrief with Claire.

Berkely: If I make it through all 20 of these dates without developing high blood pressure, it'll be a miracle.

Claire: LOL. That bad?

Berkely: That guy was crazy.

Claire: I need this whole thing made into a TV show.

Berkely: I hate everything.

She sent back a string of laughing emojis and a single word: *More.*

I groaned, tossing my phone onto the couch.

Thirteen more.

Then I was done.

For good.

Date 8

Date Eight was the kind of date that made me rethink everything—my life choices, Claire's life choices (*since this whole experiment was technically her fault*), and whether I should abandon dating altogether and take a vow of singleness.

Not that I could actually become a nun—wrong denomination.

But at this point? Even that was starting to look appealing.

His name was Ethan. On paper, he seemed great—early thirties, worked in finance, active in his church. His profile even had a C.S. Lewis quote. Promising, right?

Wrong.

I arrived at the restaurant first, grabbed a table, and waited. Five minutes passed. Then ten. Just as I started debating whether I'd been stood up, my phone buzzed.

Ethan: *Hey! I see you! Be right in.*

I glanced toward the entrance. Sure enough, there he was.

And he was standing outside.

With a selfie stick.

Taking slow-motion videos of himself.

I blinked. No. That couldn't be him. Surely not.

But then he grinned at his phone, did a final spin move, and walked inside.

Lord, give me strength.

He approached the table, setting his phone down like it was a fragile newborn. "Hey, Berkely! Great to finally meet you."

"You too," I said carefully, not mentioning the dramatic entrance.

A server came by, and we ordered. The second she left, Ethan grabbed his phone. "I hope you don't mind, but I'm documenting our date for my followers."

I choked on my water. "I—your what?"

He beamed. "I'm an influencer. My brand is 'Christian Fitness & Fire'—faith, workouts, and motivation. Got about 60K followers on TikTok. Maybe more, I haven't checked today."

Of course he hadn't. How could he? He'd been too busy recording himself slow-spinning outside a Chili's.

"That's . . . cool?" I offered, trying to catch up.

He nodded enthusiastically. "It is! People are really blessed by my content. I mean, I don't do it for the fame, obviously, but God's totally using me." He leaned in. "You'd be great for my brand, by the way."

I blinked. "Your . . . brand?"

"Yeah! You've got the look—clean-cut, classy. We could do Christian power couple content." He picked up his phone and flipped the camera on. "Here, let's give my followers a sneak peek—"

I shot out of my chair so fast, the table nearly tipped. "NOPE."

Ethan froze. "Wait, what?"

I grabbed my purse. "Ethan, you seem . . . *very into yourself*. Which is great for you. But I'd rather drink expired milk than be part of your 'Christian power couple' brand."

With that, I turned and walked straight out of the restaurant.

At home, I flopped onto the couch and Face-Timed Claire.

She answered immediately. "Well?"

I sighed. "I walked out of Chili's."

Claire gasped. "Mid-date?"

"Yes."

She cackled. "Girl, what happened?"

I rubbed my face. "He brought a selfie stick, Claire."

Silence.

Then: *wheezing laughter.*

I waited.

Finally, she gasped, "I love this for you."

I groaned. "Twelve more, Claire. Just twelve more."

And with that, I ended the call and collapsed into a pillow.

Twelve more.

Then I was done.

For good.

Date 9

I was not emotionally prepared for Date Nine.

At this point, I'd been conditioned for disaster—maybe a guy who argued about theology over dinner or someone with a pet raccoon in his car. Instead, I got Justin.

And Justin was perfect.

I walked into the Italian restaurant expecting the usual red flags and regret, but there he was—tall, nice smile, zero visible selfie sticks. He stood when I arrived, pulled out my chair, and asked me about my day.

It was unsettling.

Dinner was . . . nice? Suspiciously nice. He

made me laugh. He actually listened when I talked. When I said I liked my pasta, he casually smiled and said, "I'll have to bring you here again sometime."

And I panicked.

Not outwardly. Outwardly, I nodded and took another sip of my water. But inside? I was clawing at the walls of my soul.

Because somewhere between my second breadstick and his genuinely interesting story about his mission trip to Brazil, I felt it.

The ick.

That stupid, unexplainable, relationship-ending force that creeps in when you're with someone who is objectively wonderful but just not for you.

It made zero sense. Justin checked every box—solid faith, good career, funny, kind. The kind of guy I was supposed to want.

So why did the idea of a second date feel like a slow descent into madness?

I went home, flopped onto my couch, and texted Claire.

Berkely: Okay, now I'm mad.

Claire: What now?

Berkely: Had a GREAT date. Amazing guy. 10/10 would recommend.

Claire: I'm sorry . . . and you're MAD about this?

Berkely: YES.

Claire: . . . Do you hear yourself?

I groaned, rubbing my temples. What was wrong with me? Why couldn't I feel excited about someone who was actually decent?

My phone dinged again.

Claire: I mean, if we're being honest . . . maybe you just don't want him. Maybe you want someone else.

I stared at the screen, heart suddenly doing something weird and annoying.

I deleted the conversation. Then I locked my phone. Then I threw it across the couch like it had personally offended me.

Because, no.

Absolutely not.

Date 10

By Date Ten, I had officially hit my limit.

Not physically—I was still alive. Not emotionally—Claire's encouragement (and by encouragement, I mean relentless entertainment at my suffering) kept me going.

No, I had hit my limit in a very specific way.

A way that resulted in me going home, lying on my couch, and whispering, "I can't do this anymore."

Because Date Ten?

Was an accountant.

And I don't mean that in a normal, respectable *he-does-taxes-and-moves-on-with-his-life* kind of way.

I mean, this man lived, breathed, and evangelized Excel spreadsheets.

I should have known I was in trouble when he walked into the restaurant and the first thing he said was, *"Hope you don't mind, but I ran the numbers on this place beforehand."*

I blinked. "The numbers?"

He grinned, pulling out his phone. "Yeah, did a cost-benefit analysis based on menu pricing and serving sizes. Turns out, the best value per ounce is the chicken marsala."

I stared.

I had never wanted to go home so fast in my life.

Somehow, things only got worse.

He brought a spreadsheet to dinner. Not for work. For his personal budget.

He explained tax deductions instead of asking me about myself.

He outlined his 10-year financial projection. ("See, I plan to buy a house in three years, so if we started dating now, by the time we're engaged, the mortgage timeline would be ideal—")

He compared marriage to a mutually beneficial corporate merger.

I set my fork down slowly.

"So," I said. "You're looking for a wife . . . or a business partner?"

He laughed. "Well, ideally both! But really, marriage is about maximizing assets."

My will to live flickered.

And then. THEN.

He picked up a napkin and calculated the probability of us ending up together.
Not joking.

He actually did an equation to figure out if we were "statistically viable."

Spoiler: We were not.

Apparently, I was a financial risk.

(Which, you know what? Fair.)

Which is why, when my older brother, Grant,

invited me over for a backyard cookout that weekend, I practically sprinted out the door.

Because at this point, I needed a normal human interaction.

One that did not involve tax brackets, amortization schedules, or "maximizing assets."

When I showed up, I was immediately hit with the smell of grilled burgers and sunscreen. Grant stood behind the grill, spatula in hand, and Keagan was . . .

Also there.

Sitting on the porch steps, drinking a soda, looking annoyingly comfortable in my family's backyard.

I didn't even pause when I saw him. Keagan was just always there.

Always at our house.

Always fixing something with my dad.

Always hanging around after work.

That's what happened when you worked for my dad and your office was in the back building behind our house. You just . . . existed in our space.

Constantly.

I kicked off my sandals and flopped into a patio chair. "I need food and silence."

Grant flipped a burger. "Bad date?"

I gave him a look. "I don't even want to talk about it."

Grant laughed. "That bad?"

"Worse," I said, rubbing my temples. "He had a system for determining how compatible we were. *A literal formula.*"

Keagan raised an eyebrow. "You got math-guyed?"

"*I got math-guyed.*"

Grant whistled. "Impressive."

Keagan shook his head. "Should've told him your stats were off the charts and walked out."

I snorted before I could stop myself.

Grant glanced at me. "You know, Berk, you don't have to keep doing this to yourself. You could just, I don't know, stop dating."

Keagan nodded. "Yeah. Maybe consider that a good guy might already be right in front of you."

I looked up at him—but he wasn't looking at

me.

He was watching Grant, totally casual, totally unbothered.

I smiled, shaking my head. "You two make it sound so simple."

Keagan leaned back, grinning. "It is simple. Just find the right person."

I scoffed. "Oh, is that all? And I suppose you've got it all figured out?"

Keagan shrugged. "Hey, if I wanted a girl-friend, I could get one tomorrow."

I laughed. "Well, I'd be happy for you."

He held my gaze for a second.

Then, just smiled and took another sip of his soda.

Grant flipped a burger. "Alright, food's ready."

And just like that, the moment passed.

Date 11

I should have known this date was going to be a problem when he asked me how I felt about door-to-door work.

It started off normal enough. His name was Tyler. His profile was solid—Christian, owned his own carpet-cleaning business, loved hiking. I showed up to the coffee shop feeling cautiously optimistic.

That lasted exactly seven minutes.

"So," Tyler said, stirring his coffee, "have you ever considered door-to-door evangelism?"

I blinked. "Like . . . soliciting?"

He chuckled. "No, like sharing the good news.

Going house to house and helping people learn about the Kingdom of God."

Something in my brain clicked. "You mean, like Jehovah's Witnesses?"

He smiled. "I *am* a Jehovah's Witness."

Oh no.

I took a slow sip of my coffee. "I didn't know. Your profile just said that you were a Christian."

"I am a Christian. Jehovah's Witnesses really are the only true Christians."

"Um, actually—"

Tyler kept talking. "I just think there's something powerful about meeting people where they are, you know? Spreading the real truth about Jesus."

I hummed. "I love talking to people about Jesus, Tyler. Remind me what Jehovah's Witnesses believe about Jesus. It's been a few years since they came to my door."

His face lit up. "He's the Son of God, of course. The first created being that Jehovah made."

I tilted my head. "Created?"

Tyler nodded, like this was the most obvious thing in the world. "Yeah. He's God's first and greatest creation. He's not *God*."

Oh, it was on.

I set my coffee down and leaned forward. "Okay, but what do you do with John 20:28?"

Tyler frowned. "Huh?"

I pulled out my phone, scrolled to the verse, and turned the screen toward him. "'And Thomas answered and said to Him, '*My Lord and my God!*'" I raised an eyebrow. "Thomas literally called Jesus God."

Tyler waved a hand. "That's just a figure of speech. It doesn't mean Jesus *is* God."

I smiled sweetly. "Then why didn't Jesus correct him?"

Tyler hesitated.

I pressed on. "And what about Matthew 1:23? 'Behold, the virgin shall be with child, and bear a Son, and they shall call His name Immanuel,' which is translated, '*God with us.*'"

Tyler shifted in his seat. "Well, yeah, but that's—"

"Oh! And John 5:18." I scrolled again. "'Therefore the Jews sought all the more to kill Him, because He not only broke the Sabbath, but also said that God was His Father, making Himself *equal with God*.'" I leaned back, folding my arms. "The Jews literally wanted to kill Jesus because He was claiming to be God. And they understood Hebrew a whole lot better than we do."

Tyler's jaw clenched. "That's not what He meant."

I tilted my head. "Then why didn't He correct them?"

Tyler sighed. "Okay, wow. You're really into this, huh?"

I smiled. "I believe truth matters."

He scratched the back of his head. "Well, I'd love to talk more sometime."

I grabbed my purse. "Yeah, I don't think that's gonna happen."

Tyler frowned. "Wait, why?"

I stood. "Because we don't believe the same thing about Jesus, and that's kind of a dealbreaker for me."

His lips pressed together. "So you're seriously ending the date over doctrine?"

I smiled. "I'm ending it because my faith is the most important thing in my life, and I need someone who believes in the real Jesus."

Tyler huffed, then reached into his bag like a man with one last desperate play.

"I hear you," he said. "But I think this might change your mind."

He pulled out a copy of *The Watchtower* magazine and slid it across the table with all the gravitas of a man presenting classified government documents.

I blinked.

He nodded solemnly, like this was the theological mic drop that would turn my entire world upside down.

I glanced down at the cover.

"Is Jesus Michael the Archangel?"

I glanced back up at him.

Tyler leaned forward, eyes intense. "I'd love for you to read it and pray about it."

I exhaled slowly. "Tyler."

"Yes?"

I placed my hand on top of the magazine, gently pushed it back toward him, and said,

"I'd love for you to Google John 20:28 and pray about that."

And with that, I turned and walked straight out of the coffee shop.

That night, I flopped onto my couch and messaged Claire.

Berkely: Jehovah's Witness.

Claire: NO.

Berkely: Oh, yes.

Claire: I'm not to blame for this one. You picked him yourself on the app.

Berkely: I know. He didn't say he was a JW.

Claire: Did you get into a theological debate?

Berkely: Of course.

Claire: In the coffee shop?

Berkely: Totally.

Claire sent a string of horrified and crying face emojis in response.

Berkely: Nine more, Claire. Just nine more.

Sunday morning, I slipped into my usual pew at church, still half-dazed from the doctrinal battle royale that was Date Eleven.

The service started, but my brain refused to cooperate. Instead of listening, I found myself mentally replaying the conversation.

How had Tyler genuinely thought we might be compatible? And worse—how many people had he led to believe Jesus wasn't God?

I sighed, rubbing my forehead. This. This was why theology mattered.

The sermon wrapped up, and I barely made it out the door before I heard my name.

"Berkely!"

I turned and nearly ran straight into Keagan.

"Oh," I blurted. "Hey! Didn't see you."

He smirked. "Yeah, I got that impression."

I stepped back. "I didn't know you went here."

Keagan shrugged. "Switched churches a few months ago."

Huh. That was new.

"But I normally go to the first service."

"Ah, that's why I haven't seen you." I glanced at his Bible. "Good sermon, right?"

He nodded. "Yeah. I enjoyed learning about that archaeological discovery in Megiddo that proved the early Christians believed Jesus was God, not just some good teacher or prophet. And the early church fathers confirmed that as well in their writings. Very cool."

I blinked. "Yes! I tried to tell my date some of that stuff the other night."

Keagan's mouth quirked. "The Jehovah's Witness? Let me guess. He didn't take it well."

I sighed. "No."

Keagan chuckled. "Yeah. People don't like hearing stuff that upsets their worldview."

I tilted my head. "You know, you're kind of dangerously smart when you want to be."

He grinned. "I have my moments."

I laughed.

Then someone called his name, and he turned. "Hey, I gotta go. But I'll see you later."

He walked off, and I stood there for a second,

stomach doing something weird and annoying.

I shook it off and left, pretending I wasn't thinking about Keagan at all.

That night, Claire messaged me before I could even sit down.

Claire: You. Me. Double date. Friday.

I groaned.

Berkely: Not a chance.

Claire: It'll be fun! And this guy is actually great. I've met him before.

Berkely: He's a Christian?

Claire: Yes! I asked him.

Berkely: What's his name?

Claire: Elijah. Super sweet guy. You'll love him.

I sighed.

Berkely: Fine.

Nine more.

I tossed my phone onto the couch and closed my eyes.

Nine more.

Then I was done.

For good.

Date 12

Friday night, I pulled into the restaurant parking lot, mentally preparing for whatever fresh nonsense awaited me.

Double dates were risky. Best-case scenario? The guy was amazing, and Claire had front-row seats to my success. Worst-case? He was another disaster, and now Claire had front-row seats to my slow, painful demise.

I stepped inside, spotted Claire waving, and headed to the table.

"Berk!" she grinned. "This is Elijah."

I turned to the guy next to her—tall, friendly

smile, looked normal.

Promising.

He stood and shook my hand. "Hey, Berkely. Claire's told me a lot about you."

I smiled. "Oh yeah? Should I be concerned?"

He chuckled. "Only if half the guys she's set you up with are as bad as she says."

I laughed. "That's a low bar."

We sat down, and for the first ten minutes, things went surprisingly well. Elijah was funny, easygoing, totally normal.

I started to think, *Hey, maybe this won't be so bad.*

And that's when he said it.

"I actually have something exciting to share," he said, grinning. "I just made a huge investment in something that's gonna be big."

Claire leaned in. "Ooh, what is it?"

Elijah's grin widened. "An alpaca farm."

I froze. "A . . . what now?"

"Alpacas!" he said enthusiastically. "My buddy and I just bought land out in Colorado. It's a total game-changer. Alpaca wool is worth so much more than people realize."

I blinked. "So you . . . raise them?"

"Eventually," he said, nodding. "Right now, we're still working on securing the alpacas."

I narrowed my eyes. "Securing them," I repeated.

He waved a hand. "Yeah, just figuring out permits and zoning and all that stuff."

I turned to Claire, who was staring at her water glass like she was questioning every decision that had led her to this moment.

"Uh-huh." I nodded slowly. "And this is your . . . full-time job?"

Elijah laughed. "Oh, no, not yet. But soon! We're just waiting on the funding to come through. I've already put in most of my savings."

I choked on my drink.

Claire shot me a look of pure betrayal.

Elijah, still totally oblivious, just smiled. "What about you, Berkely? Ever thought about getting into the alpaca business?"

I set down my glass and folded my hands. "I can honestly say that in my twenty-eight years on this earth, that thought has never once crossed my mind."

Elijah grinned. "Well, maybe I can change your mind."

Lord, give me strength.

After dinner, Claire and I huddled in the parking lot, whisper-fighting.

"CLAIRE."

"I DIDN'T KNOW."

"An alpaca farm, Claire."

"I DIDN'T KNOW."

We both broke into laughter, leaning against my car.

Claire wiped her eyes. "Okay, okay. He's not the one."

I snorted. "You think?"

She sighed. "Alright, I'll find you a better one."

I groaned. "Eight more, Claire. Just eight more."

The next day, I stopped by my parents' house and, of course, Keagan was there.

I walked into the kitchen, grabbed a water, and leaned against the counter. "Hey."

Keagan, sitting at the table, raised an eyebrow. "Alpaca guy, huh?"

I whipped my head around. "HOW DO YOU KNOW THAT?"

Keagan grinned. "Your brother told me. Claire texted him."

I let out a groan. "Of course she did."

Keagan chuckled. "Hey, could've been worse. He could've tried to get you to invest."

I opened the fridge, grabbed a grape, and chucked it at him.

Keagan caught it effortlessly, popped it in his mouth, and smirked. "Better aim next time, Berk."

I sighed dramatically. "Eight more."

He tilted his head. "You sure about that?"

I rolled my eyes. "Yes, Keagan. Eight more, and I'm done."

He just smiled, taking a slow sip of his soda. "We'll see."

Date 13

Eight dates left.

At this point, I was less focused on finding love and more interested in seeing how much worse things could possibly get.

I was about to find out.

The next guy's name was Ben, and he had one of the best profiles I'd seen—loved Jesus, had a stable job, was involved in his church, and even liked dogs.

I walked into the café, for once, feeling hopeful.

Until I saw what was sitting on the table next to him.

A ventriloquist dummy.

Lord, give me strength.

Ben looked up and smiled. "Berkely, hey!"
I blinked. "Hi! Yes. Um. I see you . . . brought a guest?"

He beamed. "Oh! This is Tucker."

I stared at the tiny, dead-eyed wooden figure propped up in a chair. "Tucker."

"Yep! He comes everywhere with me."

I forced a smile, willing myself to remain calm. "Cool. You, uh . . . perform at events or something?"

Ben laughed. "Oh, no, I just love him. He's like my best friend."

I swallowed hard.

The conversation continued, but I couldn't focus. Every time I tried to listen to Ben, my eyes kept drifting to Tucker.

Sitting there.

Staring.

Ben kept talking—about his job, his faith, his

family. Honestly, he seemed pretty normal. Except for the sentient nightmare doll sitting next to him.

Halfway through my latte, Ben finally seemed to pick up on my tension.

"You're uncomfortable."

I hesitated. "No, no! I—"

He sighed. "You wouldn't believe how many girls don't give me a chance because of Tucker."

I shifted in my seat. "I mean, I—"

"Tucker, tell her how you feel." Ben reached over, lifted the dummy onto his lap, and started moving its mouth.

In a high-pitched voice, he said, "I like her, Ben! She's cute!"

I grabbed my purse and stood so fast, I nearly knocked over my chair. "You know what? I think I left my iron on."

Ben frowned. "They turn off on their own."

"Maybe. I don't know if mine does. Gotta go!" And with that, I was gone.

That night, I called Claire.

She picked up, mid-chew. "Hey! How'd it go?"

I inhaled deeply. "I got third-wheeled by a ventriloquist dummy."

Silence.

Then Claire shrieked.

I waited.

More laughter.

Finally, she gasped, "You're lying."

"I wish I was lying, Claire."

She wheezed. "No. No, I need details."

I flopped onto my couch. "He made it talk to me, Claire."

A new wave of screaming laughter.

I sighed. "Seven more. Just seven more."

Sunday afternoon, I went for a walk.

I wasn't in the mood to be social, but I needed to clear my head.

I took a deep breath, let my shoulders relax, and walked straight into Keagan.

"Oof." He caught my arms, steadying me. "You good?"

I blinked up at him. "You just appear now?

Like, out of nowhere?"

Keagan smirked. "You walked into me, Berkely."

I sighed. "I'm losing my mind."

He tilted his head. "Ventriloquist dummy guy still haunting you?"

I groaned. "I am never escaping that story, am I?"

Keagan laughed. "Not a chance."

I shook my head, but I was smiling.

He fell into step beside me, hands in his pockets. "So, seven more, huh?"

I nodded. "Seven more."

Keagan glanced at me. "And then what?"

I blinked. "What do you mean?"

"When the list is over. What then?"

I hesitated. "Then . . . I stop trying."

Keagan was quiet for a second. Then he half-smiled, like he knew something I didn't.

"Huh," he said simply.

I frowned. "What?"

"Nothing."

I stared at him. "Keagan."

His smile widened. "Nothing."

I narrowed my eyes. "I don't like you."

He chuckled. "You love me."

I snorted. "Not even close."

Keagan just grinned like he knew better.

After Keagan left, I sat in my car, staring at my steering wheel.

Seven more dates. The number of completion in the Bible. Then I was done.

I exhaled, unlocking my phone. Just as I did, Claire's name popped up.

Claire: I have a guy for you.

I groaned. Claire's *I have a guy for you* moments had a 99% failure rate.

Berkely: Please tell me he's normal.

Claire: Well. He's nice. And he's got great teeth.

I squinted at the screen.

Berkely: Why was that your second selling point?

Claire: Just trust me. Meet him tomorrow. Worst case, you hate him and we get a funny story.

I sighed, rubbing my forehead. Only seven more.

Berkely: Fine. Send me the details.

Claire: YAY.

The next evening, I arrived at the coffee shop.

I spotted him immediately—tall, blond, nice smile. Seemed normal.

I let out a relieved breath and walked over. "Hey, I'm Berkely."

He stood and shook my hand. "Nice to meet you! I'm Brigham."

I smiled. "So, Claire said you two work together."

He nodded. "Yeah, she's great."

I sat. "So, tell me about yourself."

He beamed. "Well, I just started working with Claire about two weeks ago. I've been on the mission field for the past two years."

I blinked. "Oh, cool. Like . . . overseas?"

"Nah." He took a sip of his coffee. "Just a few states over. Got to share the gospel and everything."

Something in my brain clicked.

I hesitated. "Wait. Mission trip, or . . . mission?"

He smiled. "Oh, I'm Mormon."

Oh. No.

I froze.

This was it. The moment I'd been waiting for. The Apologetics Ambush.

And I had just taken a sip of coffee, which meant I couldn't even pretend I had to leave for an emergency.

Lord, help me.

Date 14

I took a slow sip of my coffee, trying to think of a polite way to process what Brigham had just said.

Mormon.

He was Mormon.

And I was currently sipping overpriced coffee, preparing for what I could only describe as an unexpected theological showdown.

I pasted on a smile. "Oh! Wow. So . . . when you say 'share the gospel,' what exactly do you mean?"

Brigham beamed, completely oblivious to my inner crisis. "You know, helping people understand God's truth! Teaching them how they can have eternal life."

I blinked. Okay. This was happening. I set my coffee down, took a breath, and shifted into Apologetics Mode.

I smiled. "I love sharing the gospel too. So tell me—what do you think the gospel is?"

Brigham didn't hesitate. "The gospel of Jesus Christ is God's plan of happiness for us. We are all children of Heavenly Father, and He sent His Son, Jesus Christ, to atone for our sins so that we can return to live with Him. Through faith in Christ, repentance, baptism by proper authority, receiving the gift of the Holy Ghost, and enduring to the end, we can be saved. God has restored His church through a living prophet and the Book of Mormon, which testifies of Christ. By following His teachings and living righteously, we can have peace in this life and eternal life in the world to come."

"Wow." He sounded like he had said all that

about a thousand times. "So you believe that's how we're saved?"

He nodded back, clearly pleased that I understood.

I tilted my head. "Then what do you do with Ephesians 2:8–9?"

Brigham blinked. "Huh?"

I pulled out my phone, opened my Bible app, and turned the screen toward him. "It says, *For by grace you have been saved through faith, and that not of yourselves; it is the gift of God, not of works, lest anyone should boast.*"

Brigham frowned. "Well, yeah, but—"

"And what about Romans 10:9?" I continued, scrolling. "'*If you confess with your mouth that Jesus is Lord and believe in your heart that God raised him from the dead, you will be saved.*'"

Brigham shifted in his chair. "That's just part of it."

I leaned forward slightly. "But Jesus never said we had to work for our salvation. He said, '*It is finished.*'"

Brigham opened his mouth, closed it, then

chuckled. "Wow. You're really into this."

I smiled. "I believe truth matters."

He scratched the back of his head. "I mean, you're probably one of the smartest girls I've ever met, but . . ." He grinned. "You'll come around eventually."

Oh, will I? Fantastic. Nothing like a man confidently telling me I'll change my mind about the core foundation of my faith. Maybe later, he'd explain how I was also wrong about the color of the sky.

I set my coffee down and folded my hands. "Brigham, I don't think this is going to work."

His smile faltered. "Wait, what?"

I sighed, standing up. "It was nice to meet you. Really. But we don't believe the same thing about God, and that's kind of a dealbreaker for me."

Brigham let out a small laugh. "Wait, so you're really ending the date over doctrine?"

I grabbed my purse. "I'm ending it because my faith is the most important thing in my life, and I need someone who believes in the real

Jesus."

With that, I walked out of the coffee shop and into the night air, heart pounding.

Later that night, I called Claire.

She picked up on the first ring. "I'm already dying to hear this one."

I groaned, flopping onto my couch. "I just walked out of a coffee shop."

"Mid-date?"

"Yes."

"Oh my gosh." She cackled. "What happened?"

I sighed. "Mormon."

Claire gasped. "Wait—what? Brigham's Mormon?!"

"Yes! He literally thought we were on the same page!"

"Oh no."

I rubbed my forehead. "Claire. I just engaged in full-on apologetics warfare at a Starbucks."

She wheezed. "PLEASE tell me you quoted scripture at him."

"Oh, you know me. *Romans road, straight to the exit.*"

Claire howled with laughter.

I sighed. "Six more, Claire. Just six more."

And with that, I collapsed into a pillow.

Six more.

Then I was done.

For good.

Date 15

I should have known the next date was going to
be a nightmare when his opening line was:

"Life isn't about waiting for the storm to
pass—it's about learning to dance in the rain."

I blinked. "I—what?"

He smiled confidently. "It's one of my favor-
ites. It just really makes you think, you know?"

I did not know.

His name was Chad.

- He was 28, had the posture of a guy who
  had definitely read at least three self-help

books, and walked with the confidence of a man who had never questioned a single decision in his life.

- His LinkedIn profile probably said *Entrepreneur. CEO. Dream Chaser. Go-Getter.*
- And within five minutes, I had already heard:

  - "You miss 100% of the shots you don't take."
  - "Pain is just weakness leaving the body."
  - "If you aim for the moon, you'll land among the stars."

I texted Claire under the table.

Me: CLAIRE.

Claire: Oh no.

Me: HE ONLY SPEAKS IN MOTIVATIONAL QUOTES.

Claire: No.

Me: YES. LIKE, EXCLUSIVELY.

Claire: Oh, this is gonna be good.

I cleared my throat, trying to salvage a normal conversation.

"So, Chad, what do you do for work?"

He grinned. "I build businesses."

I nodded. "Oh, cool! What kind?"

He winked. "The kind that succeed."

I stared.

". . . Right. But like, what industry?"

He leaned forward. "Success isn't a destination, Berkely. It's a journey."

I blinked slowly.

"So you . . . *don't* have a job?"

He laughed. "Billionaires don't work jobs. They create opportunities."

I smiled tightly. "Right. But are you, at this present moment, making money?"

He pointed at me like I just discovered fire.

"Ah-ha! That's the mindset keeping you in a nine-to-five prison."

I texted Claire again.

Me: Claire, I think I'm on a date with a human

TED Talk.

The waiter arrived, and before I could say a word, Chad clapped his hands together.

"My man! Do you love what you do?"

The waiter blinked. "Uh . . . yeah?"

Chad nodded sagely.

"That's what it's all about. Find a job you love, and you'll never work a day in your life."

The waiter stared at him.

". . . So . . . water to start?"

Chad grinned. "I'll take whatever you recommend. Because in life, sometimes you gotta take a leap of faith."

The waiter turned to me like he needed a lifeline.

"Diet Coke," I said firmly.

Chad shook his head.

"You gotta cut out the soda, Berkely. Small habits lead to big results."

I smiled sweetly. "So does saying *no thank you.*"

I tried one last time to steer the conversation

into sanity.

"So, Chad, what do you like to do for fun?"

He pointed both index fingers at me. "Winners focus on solutions. Losers focus on problems."

I frowned. ". . . That wasn't an answer."

He nodded knowingly. "Exactly."

I stared at him.

He stared back.

The universe itself seemed to pause, trying to make sense of whatever just happened.

I reached for my phone.

Me: Claire.

Claire: Yes?

Me: He just used a motivational quote as an answer to a question.

Claire: What question?

Me: WHAT HE DOES FOR FUN.

Claire: Berk, I think you're on a date with a walking Pinterest board.

The check came, and Chad grabbed it before I could.

I smiled politely. "Oh, that's nice of you."

He winked. "The best investment you can make is in people."

I bit my lip. "So true. And I'm about to invest in leaving."

He laughed like I was kidding.

I was not kidding.

And that was the last time I let someone describe themselves as a "self-made businessman" without follow-up questions.

Date #15 – A motivational seminar in human form.

Me? Ready to never be inspired again.

Chad? Probably selling an online course somewhere.

(*Spoiler: The towel is dangerously close to being thrown in.*)

The next day, I stopped by my parents' house to steal snacks.

Keagan was there. Because of course he was.

I walked into the kitchen, grabbed a bag of

chips, and plopped down across from him at the table.

He glanced at me. "You look tired."

I ripped open the bag. "Thank you. That's exactly what a woman wants to hear."

He smirked. "Rough date?"

I sighed. "Keagan. He only spoke in motivational quotes."

Keagan blinked. "What."

"Seriously." I leaned forward.

He frowned. "Like what?"

I gestured vaguely. "There were too many. How about, *'The best way to predict the future is to create it.'*"

Keagan made a face. "That's stupid."

I pointed at him. "Right? And when I walked away to my car, he actually shouted, *'The journey of a thousand miles begins with a single step.'*"

Keagan snorted. "Wait. He didn't even walk you to your car?"

"Nope. Didn't even offer."

He shook his head. "That's a red flag. I'd definitely walk a girl to her car."

I paused mid-chip.

Then, slowly, I set the bag down. "You would. Yes! Thank you."

Keagan just took a sip of his soda, watching me. "So. Five more, huh?"

I exhaled. "Five more."

He nodded. "And if they're all disasters?"

I shrugged. "Then I'll know I gave it everything I had."

Keagan was quiet for a second.

Then, so casually I almost missed it, he said,

"Maybe the right guy's been waiting for you to figure that out."

I froze.

Brain short-circuited.

Keagan stood up like he hadn't just dropped a bomb, grabbed his keys, and stretched. "See you around, Berk."

And then he walked out the door.

I sat there, staring at nothing, brain still buffering.

What . . .

What had that been?

I shook it off and stuffed a handful of chips into my mouth. Didn't matter.

Five more.

Then I was done.

For good.

Date 16

Five more.

That's all I had left.

Five more dates, and I was free.

And if I was being honest?

I was really hoping one of them would be good.

I was so tired.

Not just of the bad dates. Not just of the Venmo requests and ventriloquist dummies and accidental apologetics debates.

I was tired of feeling like I was losing.

Claire had promised this next one would be solid.

"He's a firefighter," she had said. "He literally saves lives for a living."

Which is why, when I walked into the restaurant and saw a tall, strong, devastatingly handsome man standing at the hostess stand, I was actually excited.

I took a deep breath, straightened my shoulders, and walked up to him.

"Hi, are you Lucas?"

He turned—and wow.

Yes, Lord. This is what I'm talking about.

Lucas smiled. "Berkely?"

I grinned. "Yep!"

We sat down, ordered drinks, and within five minutes, I was sure this was going to be good.

He was funny. Confident. Had actual social skills.

I sipped my water and smiled. "So, firefighter, huh? That's amazing."

Lucas shrugged. "Yeah, it's a great job. I love it."

I nodded. "So, what made you want to do that?"

Lucas grinned. "Honestly? Women love it."

I choked on my drink.

"Excuse me?"

He laughed. "I mean, come on. It works, right? I say 'firefighter,' and look at you. You're interested."

I blinked. "I—well—I mean, I was more thinking about the *heroic, life-saving aspect,* but sure."

Lucas smirked. "Oh, yeah. That too."

My stomach sank.

No.

No, this one was supposed to be normal.

I shook it off and forced a smile. "So, uh . . . how long have you been doing it?"

"Eight years," he said. "And I love the perks. The adrenaline. The calendar."

I frowned. "The . . . what now?"

He leaned back, smirking. "You know. The firefighter calendar."

I blinked. "You mean, like . . . the scheduling system? The days off?"

"No." His smirk deepened. "The charity calendar. With all the ripped firefighter guys."

I froze. "Wait. You're in it?"

Lucas grinned. "Yup. Mister August, baby."

I stared at him like he had just confessed to being a secret international spy.

"No," I whispered.

"Oh yeah." He stretched his arms behind his head, absolutely unbothered. "Sold so many."

I leaned forward. "Lucas. Please tell me you are joking."

"Why would I joke about that?" He smirked. "It was a good month."

I rubbed my temples. "This cannot be my life."

Lucas took a sip of his drink. "Hey, when you got it, you got it."

I dropped my head onto the table.

The next morning, Claire dragged me outside for a "quick" morning bike ride.

"Sunlight is good for your mental health," she chirped as we pedaled down the path, looking far too energetic for this hour.

I yawned. "So is sleep."

Claire ignored me, glancing over. "So? How was last night's date?"

I exhaled, shaking my head. "Claire."

She grinned. "That bad?"

I shook my head. "No." Then I leveled her with a look. "Mister August."

Claire frowned. "Wait, what?"

I sighed, gripping my handlebars. "Claire. He was in a firefighter calendar. As Mister August."

Silence.

Then—a slow, breathy inhale.

I continued. "And he was so proud. Claire, he led with it."

Claire's face twitched.

"He said, 'I love my job—the adrenaline, the camaraderie . . . the calendar.'"

Claire snorted.

"And when I didn't react fast enough, he goes, 'Yeah, the firefighter calendar. With all the ripped guys. I'm Mister August, baby.'"

Claire wobbled slightly.

I pushed on. "Then he told me how many

copies they sold. He had the stats, Claire. The actual numbers."

Claire wheezed.

"He offered to sign one for me."

Claire howled, full-on losing it.

"And when I said, 'I don't own the calendar,' he winked and said, 'Not yet.'"

That did it.

Claire's body convulsed with laughter. She doubled over, wheezing so hard she could barely breathe, her whole bike shaking—

Then her handlebars wobbled.

I blinked. "Claire—"

Too late.

She lost control, swerved wildly, plowed straight through a flock of geese—

AND FELL INTO THE POND.

A feather explosion. Honking chaos.

SPLASH.

I skidded to a stop, watching as she flailed, gasping, soaked from head to toe.

A single goose stood on the bank, staring at her in pure judgment.

I wiped a hand down my face. "Four more, Claire. Just four more."

Claire, choking on laughter, lifted a water-logged hand and weakly held up a peace sign.

Later that morning, I stopped by my parents' house for coffee.

Keagan was there.

But this time?

He wasn't alone.

Sitting beside him, laughing at something he said, was a girl I had never seen before.

She was pretty.

Like, *really* pretty.

I blinked.

My mom walked into the kitchen, saw my expression, and smiled.

"Oh, Berk! Have you met Keagan's girlfriend yet?"

My stomach plummeted.

Wait.

What?

Chapter 17

I was not okay.

I had spent months suffering through the worst men in existence. I had endured Venmo requests, alpaca pitches, and a ventriloquist dummy. And now, at the eleventh hour, when I was practically crawling to the finish line . . .

Keagan had a girlfriend?

I sat in my parents' kitchen, frozen, gripping my coffee like it was the only thing tethering me to reality.

Keagan's girlfriend—who I was now realizing had a name (Olivia)—laughed again, reaching out to lightly touch his arm.

I hated it.

Wait.

No.

I did not hate it.

Because I did not care.

Because this did not matter.

I forced my face into a neutral expression, took a sip of coffee, and reminded myself of four important facts:

- Keagan was my brother's best friend.
- Keagan was allowed to date whoever he wanted.
- Keagan had asked me out once, and I said no. And most importantly . . .
- I was four dates away from being done with dating forever.

I cleared my throat. "So. Olivia."

She turned to me, all bright eyes and blinding friendliness. "Yes! You're Berkely, right? Keagan's told me so much about you."

I smiled back. "Has he?"

Keagan—who had been watching me carefully this whole time—took a sip of *not soda* for once, thank you very much.

Olivia nodded enthusiastically. "Oh yeah! He told me you were doing that whole '20 dates' thing. How's that going?"

My jaw clenched.

"Oh, great," I said lightly. "I've met some fascinating people."

Keagan coughed into his drink.

Olivia grinned. "That's so fun! I could never do something like that. I'm just so picky."

My eye twitched.

I smiled harder.

Keagan hid his smirk behind his mug.

I turned to him. "So, how long have you two been together?"

Keagan's smirk faded.

Olivia beamed. "Just a couple of weeks, but it's been amazing. He's so great."

My stomach twisted.

No.

Nope.

Absolutely not.

I was not jealous.

I was totally fine.

Because this was Keagan.

And Keagan was not my problem.

I pushed back my chair. "Well, I'd love to stay and chat, but I actually have another date tonight."

Keagan's grip tightened around his mug.

Olivia lit up. "Oh, that's exciting! Who's the guy?"

I blinked. "Uh."

I didn't actually know. Claire had set it up.

I pulled out my phone and checked my messages.

Berkely: Who am I meeting tonight?

Claire: James. Super solid guy. No weird hobbies. Promise.

I looked back up. "His name's James."

Olivia clapped her hands together. "Ooh, I hope it goes well!"

Keagan said nothing.

I grabbed my coffee and walked out.

Later that night, I met James.

And he was . . .

Perfect.

Handsome. Kind. Funny. The type of guy who would never, in a million years, try to sell me an alpaca timeshare or carry a ferret in his hoodie.

And yet?

I wasn't present at all.

Because I couldn't stop hearing Olivia's voice in my head.

Keagan's so great.

I stirred my tea absentmindedly.

James smiled. "You okay?"

I forced a laugh. "Yeah! Sorry, long day."

He nodded. "I get that."

I mentally shook myself.

No.

I was not going to ruin this date because of Keagan.

James was exactly what I had been looking for.

So why did I feel like I had just lost something?

Date 17

I was not thinking about Keagan.

Nope. Not even a little bit.

I was absolutely, one hundred percent thinking about James.

Because James was handsome. James was smart. James was basically a Hallmark movie love interest in human form.

And yet.

When Claire walked into the apartment and flopped onto the couch beside me, she nudged my knee. "Sooo? How did it go?"

The first words out of my mouth were: "Keagan has a girlfriend."

Claire froze mid-reach for the remote.

Then, slowly, she turned to face me. "I . . . meant your date?"

I blinked. "Oh. Right. Yeah. James was great. Super nice."

Claire squinted. "But?"

I hesitated.

There was no but.

Except for the tiny, inconvenient, massive but.

The Keagan-sized but.

I shoved a throw pillow over my face and groaned. "Keagan has a girlfriend."

Claire yanked the pillow away and held it in her lap. "Oh, honey."

I sat up. "No. Do not 'oh, honey' me! This does not matter. I do not care. I am simply stating a fact."

She just stared at me.

I crossed my arms. "What."

"You are spiraling."

I scoffed. "I am fine."

Claire slowly raised an eyebrow.

I stood, threw my arms out dramatically. "I

AM THRIVING."

Claire snorted. "Oh, for sure."

I pointed at her. "Shut up."

She barely contained her smirk. "Sooo . . . you're gonna see James again?"

I froze.

Then I did the only logical thing.

I deflected.

"I actually have another date tonight."

Claire blinked. "Wait, you're still stacking them?"

I flopped back onto the couch. "I have a system, Claire."

She sighed. "Fine. Who's this one?"

I grabbed my phone off the coffee table and checked my messages.

"His name's Zayn. Super solid guy. No weird hobbies."

Claire wiggled her eyebrows. "Ooh. Sounds promising."

I forced a smile. "Yep. I'm sure it'll be great."

Claire grinned. "Oh yeah. That face just screams 'romantic optimism.'"

I chucked the throw pillow at her head. She dodged it, laughing.

Date 18

By Date Eighteen, I was hanging on by a thread.

I was mentally exhausted. Spiritually drained. And most of all?

I was completely and totally fine about Keagan having a girlfriend.

Nope. Not thinking about it at all.

Which is why, when I walked into the café and spotted my next date, I was determined to be upbeat.

I saw him near the window—clean-cut, good posture, normal-looking.

Promising.

I smiled as I approached. "Hey! You must be Zayn."

He stood, grinning. "Yes! Great to meet you, Berkely."

We shook hands, sat down, and ordered our drinks.

"So," I started, "my friend at work said you go to church in town?"

Zayn tilted his head. "Um . . . sort of."

"Oh?"

He smiled. "It's the mosque on Fifth. Not exactly a church."

I blinked.

I smiled politely. "Oh! Um . . . sorry, I thought she said you were Christian?"

He nodded. "Well, they're really not that different. I mean, I believe in Jesus."

I stared. "As the Son of God?"

He laughed. "Oh, no. That's where Christians got confused. Jesus was just a great prophet."

I inhaled sharply.

Welp. I'm about to do full-blown apologetics over a macchiato.

I shifted my chair like I was queuing up a PowerPoint slide.

Took a slow sip. Collected my entire being. Then smiled. "So, fun fact about that. . ."

Thirty minutes later, Zayn was not having fun anymore.

"But the Bible's been changed," he insisted.

I shook my head. "Nope. We have over 5,800 early manuscripts of the New Testament, all confirming the same message."

He frowned. "Well, Paul was the one who invented the idea that Jesus was God."

I pulled up John 8:58. "No. In the Gospel of John—written by one of the original twelve disciples, an eyewitness to Jesus's life—Jesus calls Himself 'I AM,' the same name God used in Exodus. In 2 Peter 1:1, the apostle Peter called Jesus 'our God and Savior.'"

Zayn crossed his arms. "But the Quran says—"

I leaned forward. "When was the Quran written?"

He hesitated. "Uh . . . like 600 years later?"

"Exactly. And Jesus already warned us that false prophets would come after Him." I showed him Matthew 24:24. "If Jesus Himself said He was God, and people wrote it down within their lifetime, who should I believe—a firsthand account or something written six centuries later?"

Zayn shifted uncomfortably. "I mean . . . I don't know."

I smiled. "That's okay. Just don't let anyone tell you Jesus didn't claim to be God. Because He did."

After the date, I called Claire.

She answered immediately. "PLEASE tell me this one was normal."

I sighed. "It turned into an apologetics debate instead of a date."

Silence.

Then: "EXCUSE ME??"

I flopped onto the couch. "Claire. He was Muslim."

Claire shrieked.

"HOW?!"

"My friend at work thought he was a Christian because he believed in the power of prayer."

Claire was crying laughing. "I—WHAT?? Prayer?"

"Yeah, five times a day facing Mecca."

"Oh no."

I sighed. "And obviously, I couldn't just let it go. So now, I've spent the last hour defending the Bible's reliability over coffee."

More screeching laughter.

I rubbed my face. "Two dates left, Claire, and this challenge is over."

Claire snorted. "And yet somehow, I feel like you're in crisis."

I frowned. "I'm not in crisis."

Claire cackled. "You sure? Because you sound a little like someone realizing they only have two dates left to meet their husband."

I froze.

Wait.

WAIT.

No.

That was not what was happening.

I was totally fine.

Claire just hummed knowingly.

I groaned. "I AM IN COMPLETE CON-TROL, CLAIRE."

She wheezed. "Oh, sweetie. You are absolutely not."

I ignored her.

Two more.

Just two more.

The next day, I stopped by my parents' house to pretend to be a normal, functioning human.

Keagan was there.

Of course he was.

And this time?

Olivia was sitting in his lap.

I froze.

Keagan spotted me and immediately stiffened, like he'd been caught doing something illegal.

Olivia, oblivious, just smiled. "Oh, hi, Berkely!"

I smiled back, ignoring the fact that my stomach felt like it had just dropped into my shoes.

I did not care.

I was fine.

Totally fine.

I cleared my throat. "Hey, I was just grabbing—uh—something."

Keagan did not take his eyes off me.

I walked to the kitchen, grabbed a banana (why a banana? I don't know, it was there), and walked back out.

Keagan was still watching me.

I refused to look at him.

Instead, I smiled at Olivia.

"You two are adorable," I said brightly, peeling my pointless banana.

Keagan's jaw tightened.

Olivia beamed. "Aw, thank you! He's just the best."

I took a huge bite of banana so I wouldn't say something regrettable.

Keagan stood up abruptly. "Hey, Berk, can I talk to you for a sec?"

I swallowed hard. "Oh, uh, I was just leaving."

He narrowed his eyes slightly. "It'll just take a second."

I hesitated.

Then I stuffed the rest of the banana in my mouth and nodded.

Keagan walked me outside.

I turned to him. "What?"

He looked at me for a long moment.

Then, very slowly, he said, "Are you okay?"

I stared.

"I—yes? Why wouldn't I be?"

Keagan's jaw ticked. "I don't know. You tell me."

My heart pounded.

I scoffed. "Keagan. I am *thriving.*"

He exhaled, running a hand through his hair. "Berk, if—"

I held up a hand.

"I'm fine," I said brightly. "Two more dates, and I'm done! Then I can relax and never think about dating again."

Keagan's expression darkened.

For a second, I thought he was going to say something else.

But then he just nodded once, clipped. "Right."

I turned on my heel and walked away.

I did not look back.

Because I was totally, completely fine.

Right?

Date 19

Two more.

Just two more.

And then?

Freedom.

I had made it through eighteen dates, and somehow, I was still standing. I had survived free dessert hustlers, calendar models, lice, and wooden dummies. I had endured.

And now, I just needed to make it through two more dates.

Then, I would never have to think about dating again.

Ever.

Which is why, as I walked into the restaurant, I felt light.

Carefree.

I was about to be done.

And then I saw my date.

And the light feeling vanished.

Because I knew, instantly, that this one was going to be a nightmare.

He was already seated, scrolling on his phone.

He had AirPods in.

AirPods.

On a first date.

I almost turned around right then.

But no.

I had come this far. I was finishing this.

I walked up, smiled, and said, "Hey! You must be Jared."

He did not look up.

I blinked.

"Um . . . hi?"

Still nothing.

I awkwardly cleared my throat.

Finally, he glanced up, removed one AirPod,

and said, "Huh?"

I smiled tightly. "Are you Jared?"

"Yeah," he said flatly. "Hold on."

And then?

He put his finger up.

As in, *hold on, I'm finishing something.*

As in, *I was being asked to wait.*

On my own date.

I stared.

I waited.

And then, after a solid twenty seconds, he sighed dramatically, put his phone down, and said, "Sorry, my fantasy draft is insane right now."

Lord.

Give me strength.

I sat down, mentally counting to ten.

"Right. So! Uh, tell me a little about yourself."

Jared leaned back, completely relaxed. "Not much to tell. I work in sales. I hit the gym. Play fantasy football. Pretty chill life."

I waited.

That was it?

That was his entire personality?

I forced a smile. "Cool! So, um . . . what do you like to do outside of work?"

He shrugged. "Mostly gym and fantasy."

I nodded slowly. "Right. And . . . church?"

He squinted at me. "What about it?"

I blinked. "Well. Do you go?"

Jared frowned like he was confused by the question. "Yeah, I mean. When I have time."

I waited.

Hoped he would elaborate.

He did not.

I took a sip of water, contemplating my life choices.

Then, trying one more time, I said, "So, what kind of things are you looking for in a relationship?"

Jared grinned. "Oh, you know. Just a cool girl. Chill. Not too high-maintenance."

I stared.

That was it.

That was his whole answer.

And then?

Something in me snapped.

Because suddenly, I was exhausted.

Not just by *this* date.

By all of them.

By the whole thing.

I had spent months chasing this imaginary finish line, thinking that if I just kept going, I might find what I was looking for.

But what if I had already passed it?

What if I had already walked right by it without even realizing?

My stomach twisted.

I didn't want to be here.

Not just on *this* date.

On any date.

I wanted to be somewhere else.

With someone else.

I stiffened.

No.

No, that wasn't—

Jared was still talking.

I snapped back to reality just in time to hear him say, "So, what are you looking for?"

I opened my mouth.

And nothing came out.

Because I didn't know anymore.

I didn't know what I was looking for.

But I knew who I wasn't looking for.

And he was sitting right in front of me.

I swallowed hard, pushed back my chair, and stood.

Jared blinked. "Wait—where are you going?"

I grabbed my purse.

"I'm sorry," I said. "But I—I can't do this."

And then?

I walked out of the restaurant.

But I didn't feel relief.

I felt empty.

For the first time in months, I wasn't frustrated or annoyed or even angry at men in general.

I was just tired.

I climbed into my car, shut the door, and just sat there.

Staring.

Numb.

This was supposed to feel good.

I was supposed to walk away from this date feeling free.

But all I felt was . . .

Like I had lost something.

I shook my head, forcing the thought away.

No.

I was fine.

I was just burnt out. That was all.

One more.

Just one more.

Then I was done.

The next day, I stopped by my parents' house for coffee.

Keagan was there.

Because of course he was.

But this time?

He was alone.

No Olivia.

Just Keagan, sitting at the kitchen table, scrolling through his phone.

He glanced up when I walked in. "Hey."

I nodded. "Hey."

Then I poured my coffee and sat across from him.

Silence.

I stared at my mug.

He stared at his phone.

Finally, I cleared my throat. "No Olivia today?"

Keagan hesitated. "Nah. She's busy."

I took a sip. "Cool, cool."

More silence.

Then, casually, Keagan said, "So. Mister AirPods, huh?"

I froze.

My eyes snapped to his.

Keagan smirked. "Claire texted Grant, who texted me."

I groaned. "WHY DOES EVERYONE KNOW MY LIFE?!"

Keagan laughed. "Because it's hilarious."

I glared. "I'm gonna need you to pretend this conversation never happened."

Keagan grinned. "Not a chance."

I sighed dramatically. "This is the worst timeline."

Keagan just watched me, amusement flickering in his eyes.

And then, so casually I almost missed it, he said,

"You could just stop, you know."

I blinked. "What?"

Keagan shrugged. "The dating thing. You don't have to keep doing this."

I frowned. "I made a deal with myself. I'm seeing it through."

Keagan nodded slowly. "Right. Because quitting would be, what, admitting something?"

My stomach flipped.

I forced a laugh. "Keagan, I—"

He held up a hand. "Forget it. Just . . . think about it."

I stared at him, grabbed my coffee, and stood. "One more."

Keagan just smiled.

And for some reason?

It bothered me.

Date 20

One more.

That was it.

I had spent months suffering through the absolute worst men in existence. I had endured everything from ventriloquist dummies to Mr. August. And now?

I was so close to the finish line.

Just one more date.

I should have felt relief.

Instead, I felt unsettled.

Claire had hyped up this guy like crazy.

"This is it, Berk," she had said. "This is the one."

So when I walked into the café and saw my date waiting at the counter, I actually felt a flicker of hope.

He was tall, clean-cut, well-dressed. Looked normal.

I inhaled deeply, shoved every stray Keagan thought out of my brain, and walked up to him.

"Hi! You must be Noah."

He turned, smiled, and—

Wow.

Okay.

Noah was ridiculously good-looking. The kind of guy who probably builds furniture in his spare time just for fun.

He stood, shook my hand, and said, "Berkely. Nice to finally meet you."

His voice was deep. Calm. Steady.

The kind of voice that made you feel like this man never forgets to pay his taxes.

I sat down, already optimistic.

He smiled. "Claire told me a little about you."

I grinned. "And you still showed up?"

He chuckled. "I like a woman with a plan."

Hope skyrocketed.

The date started, and within ten minutes, I was completely into it.

He was kind.

He was funny.

He was actually interested in my faith.

He asked about my job, my family, my favorite places to travel.

He loved Jesus. He was actually listening. He was NOT IN A CALENDAR.

And then?

Halfway through my drink, he looked at me and said, "So . . . what are you looking for?"

I froze.

For the first time in this whole process, that question threw me off.

Because usually?

I knew the answer.

But suddenly, my brain glitched.

Because instead of thinking about Noah . . .

I was thinking about Keagan.

My stomach twisted.

No.

I shook the thought away.

This was exactly what I had planned for.

Noah was exactly the kind of guy I had been hoping to find.

So why did it feel like I was sitting in the wrong restaurant?

With the wrong person?

My chest tightened.

I took a sip of water and tried to get it together.

Noah tilted his head. "You okay?"

I forced a smile. "Yeah! Just a long week."

He nodded, completely unaware that my whole world was quietly falling apart.

I barely made it out of the restaurant before the first tear fell.

I hurried to my car, climbed inside, and just sat there.

Heart pounding.

Hands gripping the steering wheel.

Vision blurring.

This was supposed to be over.

This was supposed to feel like relief.

But instead?

It felt like my chest was caving in.

Because suddenly, I saw it.

I saw every time Keagan made me laugh when I was trying to be mad.

I saw every casual touch that had felt so normal . . . but wasn't.

I saw every dumb inside joke, every glance across the room, every moment that had been so obvious—but I had been too blind to see it.

And then?

I saw Olivia.

I saw her sitting in his lap.

I saw her laughing at his jokes.

I saw him looking at her the way I should have let him look at me.

My breath hitched.

And then, very quietly, I broke.

I pressed my forehead against the steering wheel, squeezed my eyes shut, and let the silent sobs shake my entire body.

Because I had finally figured it out.

I had finally realized the truth.

And it was too late.

I woke up the next morning with puffy eyes, a pounding headache, and the sinking realization that my life was in shambles.

I had wasted months chasing something I already had.

And now?

It was gone.

I ignored Claire's texts. I skipped church. I stayed in my apartment like some tragic, post-breakup cliché, even though I hadn't actually been with Keagan.

But it felt like I had lost him.

And that was somehow worse.

By Sunday evening, Claire had had enough.

She let herself into my room with a smoothie in one hand and pure judgment in her eyes.

"Okay. This is pathetic."

I glared. "You have no authority here."

She tossed the smoothie at me. "Drink. You look dehydrated."

I caught it but did not drink.

Claire sat across from me. Folded her arms. "You realize what you have to do, right?"

I looked away. "Nope."

Claire tilted her head. "Berkely."

I took a very aggressive sip. "There is nothing to do."

Claire sighed dramatically. "I swear, you are the most stubborn person I've ever met."

I set the smoothie down. "What do you want me to say, Claire? That I ruined everything? That I made a huge mistake and now I have to live with it?"

She blinked. "Well. Yes."

I huffed.

Claire leaned forward. "Look, you have two options. You can either sit here and cry into your overpriced smoothie—"

"Rude."

"—or you can fight for him."

I froze.

My stomach twisted.

Because that wasn't an option.

Not really.

I shook my head. "He's with Olivia."

Claire rolled her eyes. "So?"

I stared at her. "So?! I missed my chance."

Claire exhaled slowly.

And then she said, "Maybe. But maybe not."

I stiffened.

Claire's voice softened. "Berk . . . what if he's just waiting for you to finally figure it out?"

My heart pounded.

No.

That wasn't—

That couldn't be—

Could it?

I swallowed hard. "I don't know."

Claire tilted her head. "Well. Maybe it's time to find out."

Chapter 21

I had never been so nervous in my entire life.

Not when I took my first job interview.

Not when I had to do an apologetics debate over coffee.

Not even when I found out Mister August was a real person.

No.

This was worse.

Because I wasn't just walking into this conversation to talk.

I was walking in to lose.

Either I was going to lose Keagan to Olivia for good . . .

Or I was going to lose my pride and finally tell him the truth.

Either way?

I was walking away with nothing left to hide behind.

I pulled into his driveway and turned off the car.

The house was dark, except for the porch light.

I sat there for a full thirty seconds, gripping the steering wheel, my pulse hammering in my ears.

I could leave.

I could pretend this never happened, drive home, and let Keagan be happy with Olivia.

I could—

No.

I exhaled sharply.

I got out.

I walked to the door.

And I knocked.

Keagan answered almost immediately.

And for a second, we just stood there.

His blue eyes flicked over me, confused, cautious. "Berkely?"

I swallowed hard. "Hey."

Keagan hesitated. "Are you okay?"

I almost laughed.

No.

No, I was not okay.

I had spent the last six months wrecking my own life. I had walked past every single red flag, neon sign, and God-sent wake-up call screaming YOU LOVE HIM, and I had ignored every single one.

And now I was here.

And I had no idea what to say.

So I just blurted it out.

"I was wrong."

Keagan blinked. "About?"

I inhaled deeply.

And then, in barely more than a whisper, I said, "You."

Keagan froze.

I pressed on before I lost my nerve.

"I was wrong about you. And us. And all of this." I gestured vaguely between us, my chest aching. "I spent all this time looking for something I already had, and I—I didn't even see it."

Keagan's jaw tightened.

And then, very carefully, he said,

"I don't know what you want me to say, Berkely."

I stumbled over my words. "I—I just—"

Keagan let out a slow breath, raking a hand through his hair.

"I waited for you," he said.

The words were soft. Controlled. But underneath them, I could hear the weight of everything he wasn't saying.

"I waited for you to figure it out. I waited for you to see me." He exhaled sharply, shaking his head. "But you never did."

My chest cracked open.

"I see you now," I whispered.

Keagan's jaw ticked.

And then, voice rough, he said,

"You're too late."

The words hit like a gut punch.

I stared at him, my throat burning, my hands shaking at my sides.

"No," I whispered.

Keagan shook his head. "Berk—"

"No." My voice rose this time, desperate, raw. "Don't do that. Don't just—don't just shut me out like that."

Keagan's expression hardened. "What do you want me to do, Berkely?" His voice was sharp now. "You decided I wasn't worth it. And now that I'm with someone else, you suddenly change your mind?"

I winced. "That's not fair—"

"It's completely fair," he cut in. "You got to make your choice. And I had to move on."

Tears burned my eyes.

I had known this might happen. I had known that showing up tonight was a risk.

But I hadn't been prepared for this.

For him being mad at me.

For him being done.

Keagan exhaled, shaking his head. "I can't do

this, Berkely."

Something inside me snapped.

"Can't do what, Keagan?" My voice shook, my hands curling into fists. "Have a single conversation with me? After all these years, you can't even—"

"I can't do this again," he interrupted, his voice low and strained.

I froze.

Keagan swallowed hard, his throat working. "I asked you out once. And you said no." His hands clenched. "Do you have any idea what that felt like?"

I swallowed hard.

"I—I didn't think you really cared," I admitted, voice barely above a whisper. "You acted like it didn't even bother you."

Keagan let out a sharp, humorless laugh. "Because what was I supposed to do, Berkely? Beg you to change your mind?"

I looked away.

Because the truth was?

I had never thought about it like that.

Keagan shook his head. "You didn't want me then. And I don't know if I can trust that you want me now."

My vision blurred.

"Keagan." My voice cracked. "I know I messed up. I know I waited too long, I know I don't deserve this. But. . ." I exhaled unsteadily.

And then, with everything in me, I whispered,

"I love you."

Silence.

Keagan's expression cracked.

His chest rose and fell unevenly.

But he didn't say anything.

He just stood there.

And I realized—

I was too late.

My throat closed.

I turned away before I completely fell apart.

"Forget it," I whispered. "I shouldn't have come."

I started walking.

One step.

Two.

Three.

And then—

His hand caught my wrist.

I froze.

My breath hitched.

And then—

Very, very softly—

Keagan whispered,

"Say it again."

I turned back.

Slowly.

Keagan's blue eyes burned into mine.

His grip tightened on my wrist.

And I knew.

I wasn't too late.

I exhaled.

And then, with everything in me, I whispered,

"I love you."

And then his mouth was on mine.

Chapter 22

Keagan kissed me like he'd been waiting his whole life for this moment.

Like he had been holding back for years—and now, finally, he didn't have to.

His hands slid into my hair, pulling me closer, deeper, like he was afraid I'd disappear if he let go.

And I kissed him back with everything in me.

Because I had finally found what I'd been searching for.

And it had been him all along.

When we finally pulled apart, Keagan's forehead rested against mine, his breathing uneven.

I couldn't stop staring at him.

His blue eyes were softer now, searching mine, like he was still trying to believe this was real.

Like he was afraid he was going to wake up and this would all be a dream.

I reached up and brushed my fingers against his jaw.

"I'm so sorry," I whispered.

Keagan's eyes flickered with something unreadable.

I swallowed hard. "I didn't mean to hurt you."

His jaw tensed. "But you did."

I nodded. "I know."

Keagan ran a hand through his hair. "And when you said no . . . I told myself I'd be fine. That it was no big deal. That we could just go back to being friends." He let out a humorless chuckle. "But I was lying."

My chest tightened.

I bit my lip. "Why didn't you tell me?"

Keagan looked at me like I had just asked him if the sky was blue.

"Because I didn't want you to be with me out

of guilt, Berkely." His voice was gravelly, like the words had been locked up inside him for years. "I didn't want to be your backup plan. I wanted to be your first choice."

I felt my stomach drop.

Because that's exactly what I had done.

I had pushed him aside. Looked right past him while searching for something else.

Something that had never even existed.

I blinked back tears. "You were always my first choice," I whispered. "I was just too blind to see it."

Keagan was quiet for a long time.

Then, finally, he exhaled.

I hesitated. "What about Olivia?"

He let out a slow exhale.

And then, very softly, he said, "She broke up with me."

I stilled.

My heart pounded. "When?"

Keagan hesitated. "Two days ago."

I inhaled sharply. "Why?"

Keagan swallowed hard.

Then, barely above a whisper, he said, "She read my journal."

I blinked. "What?"

Keagan let out a slow breath. "It was on my nightstand. She picked it up . . . and she read it." He dragged a hand through his hair, shaking his head. "She saw everything I wrote about you."

My stomach twisted.

I whispered, "What did it say?"

Keagan exhaled.

Then, his voice hoarse, raw, barely more than a breath, he said, "That I love Berkely Monroe. That I've loved you for years."

The air left my lungs.

My knees went weak, my chest tightened, my pulse hammered so hard I could feel it in my throat.

He had written it down.

Not just once. Not just some fleeting thought.

He had loved me for years.

Keagan ran a hand down his face. "She didn't even get mad. She just looked at me and said, 'I deserve better than being second place in my own relationship.'" He exhaled sharply. "And she was right."

A lump formed in my throat.

"She knew," I whispered. "She knew before I did."

Keagan swallowed hard. "I think everyone did."

Tears blurred my vision.

Keagan reached up, cupped my face in his hands, and looked me right in the eyes.

"But it was never her," he whispered.

A single tear slipped down my cheek.

"Then why did you stay with her?" I asked.

Keagan sighed. "Because I didn't think you were ever going to see me, Berk." He let out a soft, breathless laugh. "And I had to stop hoping you would."

I let out a quiet sob. "I see you now."

Keagan's blue eyes darkened.

And then, in barely more than a whisper, he said,

"Then prove it."

Chapter 23

Keagan had told me to prove it.

So I did.

The next night, I showed up at his house with groceries.

Keagan blinked at me from the doorway. "What's this?"

I lifted the bags. "Dinner."

His eyebrows lifted. "You're cooking for me?"

I brushed past him into the kitchen. "I seem to recall you once saying that acts of service was your love language."

Keagan leaned against the counter, smirking. "You remembered that?"

I glanced at him over my shoulder. "Keagan, I remember everything."

His smirk faded.

Something warmer flickered in his eyes.

I turned back to the stove before I melted completely.

An hour later, Keagan took one bite and nearly fell out of his chair.

"Berkely." His eyes widened. "What is this?"

I grinned. "Homemade carbonara."

Keagan stabbed another bite. "Where did you learn to cook like this?"

I shrugged. "It's called YouTube."

Keagan laughed. "You learned this for me?"

I smirked. "Well, I certainly didn't learn it for Olivia."

Keagan nearly choked.

On Sunday morning, I showed up at the early church service, the one he attends.

Keagan was already sitting down when I slid into the seat next to him.

He glanced over, surprised. "You came to the

first service?"

I nudged his knee with mine. "Where else would I be?"

Keagan stared at me for a long second.

Then, slowly, he reached over and laced his fingers through mine.

I didn't let go.

That night, I did something I had never done before.

I posted a picture of Keagan on Instagram.

It wasn't fancy—just a shot of him laughing at dinner, caught in a genuinely happy moment.

The caption?

"Some people just make life better" with a heart emoji.

It wasn't much.

But it was enough.

Claire called thirty seconds later.

"BERKELY."

I grinned. "Hey, Claire."

"NO. You do not just soft-launch your relationship like this and expect me to act like a normal person."

I laughed. "He's not a secret."

Claire screeched. "SO IT'S TRUE??"

"Yes."

"YOU'RE IN LOVE WITH KEAGAN?"

"Yes."

"HE'S IN LOVE WITH YOU?"

"Yes."

"YOU'RE GOING TO MARRY HIM?"

I froze.

Claire gasped. "OH MY GOSH, YOU ARE."

I covered my face. "I cannot talk to you."

Claire cackled. "I AM PLANNING YOUR BRIDAL SHOWER."

And then she hung up.

Chapter 24

Six Months Later . . .

I used to think that falling in love would feel like fireworks.

Like some big, dramatic moment where everything suddenly made sense.

But love wasn't a single moment.

It was thousands of tiny ones.

It was Keagan saving me the last piece of pizza even when he wanted it.

It was him texting me goodnight every night, even if we'd been together all day.

It was him praying for me—out loud, unprompted, as if it was the most natural thing in the world.

It was time. Growth. Commitment.

And it was the easiest, most obvious thing in my life.

The past six months had been full of firsts.

- First official date. (He took me stargazing and made me hot chocolate. I cried.)
- First time saying 'I love you' without fear. (He said it first. I said it louder.)
- First serious fight. (We argued about how much soda is *too much* soda. Claire refereed.)
- First trip together. (We visited my brother in Texas. Keagan was a *champ* at handling my chaotic family.)
- First time he told me he wanted to marry me. (We were sitting in church. He just . . . leaned over and said it. Like a promise.)

And now?

Now, I knew without a doubt that he was my

future.

The only question was . . .

When would he ask me to be his wife?

I was at my parents' house when it happened.

It was a normal Sunday afternoon.

Mom was baking. Dad was watching football.
Claire was texting me *unhinged* wedding ideas—

(*"Berk, what if you and Keagan have a fireworks exit? But like, BIGGER than normal fireworks? Like, a full-on Fourth of July show??"*)

I was about to reply when my phone buzzed with a new text.

Keagan: Come outside.

I frowned.

Berkely: I'm in sweatpants.

Keagan: You'll be fine.

I rolled my eyes but grabbed my hoodie and slipped outside.

Keagan was standing by his truck.

And he looked nervous.

I blinked. "Keagan?"

He smiled. But it wasn't his normal, teasing

smile. It was . . . different.

Softer.

Sweeter.

My stomach fluttered.

Keagan stepped forward, reaching for my hands.

I let him take them, my heart racing.

And then, very quietly, he said,

"I love you, Berk."

I exhaled. "I love you too."

Keagan's thumb brushed over my knuckles.

And then—

He reached into his jacket pocket.

Pulled out a small, velvet box.

And dropped to one knee.

My breath caught.

My hands flew to my mouth.

And then Keagan, voice full of absolute certainty, said:

"Berkely, I have loved you for years. I've waited for you, I've fought for you, and I will never stop choosing you."

He opened the box.

A ring sparkled inside.

"Marry me?" he whispered.

My eyes burned.

My chest ached.

And for the first time in my life, I didn't hesitate.

"Yes."

Keagan's face broke into a grin.

He slid the ring onto my finger, then pulled me into his arms and kissed me like I was his whole world.

Because I was.

And he was mine.

For the rest of our lives.

Chapter 25

The moment I walked back inside, Claire tackled me.

"DID IT HAPPEN?" she screeched.

I held up my hand. "It happened."

Claire screamed. My mom gasped. My dad paused the game.

Then suddenly, I was being pulled into hugs, my ring was being admired from every angle, and Claire was already pulling up Pinterest.

"Oh my gosh," she whispered. "This is happening. This is actually happening."

I laughed. "Claire—"

"No, no. I need a moment." She grabbed my hands, eyes shining. "I told you this would happen. I knew this would happen. And now I get to plan the most *epic* wedding in history."

I blinked. "Wait—"

Claire grinned. "Berkely. Strap in. You're about to enter wedding planning chaos."

Three Months Before the Wedding . . .

Keagan and I sat in a coffee shop, staring at our wedding planning list.

It was long.

Very, *very* long.

Keagan took a sip of his drink. "So, tell me again why Claire is in charge of everything?"

I sighed. "Because Claire thrives in chaos. This is her dream job."

Keagan grinned. "I'm pretty sure she thinks it's *her* wedding."

I groaned. "Keagan, she suggested a *live lion* as part of the entrance."

Keagan choked on his coffee. "I beg your

pardon?"

I rubbed my temples. "Her exact words were, 'Think Daniel in the lion's den, but make it bridal.'"

Keagan laughed. "That is so Claire."

I set down my pen. "Okay. Important question. What do you actually care about for the wedding?"

Keagan thought for a second. "Food."

I nodded. "Good call."

"And you."

My heart flipped. "Keagan."

He shrugged, smirking. "As long as you walk down that aisle, I don't care if there's a lion or fireworks or even Mister August standing in the background."

I burst out laughing. "Okay, well, let's *not* have Mister August."

Keagan grinned. "Then I guess we're good."

The Wedding Day . . .

I had never been so happy in my life.

The morning was a blur of laughter, prayer, and Claire running around like a general leading an army.

But the moment I walked down the aisle, everything stopped.

Because there was Keagan.

Waiting.

Smiling.

Looking at me like I was the best decision he'd ever made.

And when I reached him, he leaned in and whispered, "Took you long enough."

Then, quieter, *softer*—so only I could hear— he added, "I'd have waited forever."

I laughed.

And then, in front of everyone we loved, we promised a lifetime together.

The Honeymoon in Israel . . .

The first night in Israel, we sat on a balcony overlooking the Sea of Galilee.

Keagan had his arm around me. The water sparkled with the reflection of the stars.

And I thought—

This is it.

This is everything I've ever wanted.

Keagan kissed my forehead. "Worth the wait?"

I smiled. "Every second."

And for the first time in my life, I didn't feel like I was waiting for something.

I was exactly where I was meant to be.

With exactly the person I was meant to love.

For the rest of my life.

Thanks for reading!
I'd love to hear your feedback. Email me at
Charlie@AlwaysBeReady.com

If you enjoyed this book, you'll
love the companion novel:

20 Dates & I'm Doomed
Think dating is rough for women?
Meet Caleb. His ex just set him up
. . . and it's going terribly.

She was sent to expose him. Now they're running for their lives. Kate Lawson, a top undercover spy, is assigned to uncover the dark secrets of a powerful pastor. But James Caldwell isn't the man her handlers claim he is— and refusing to take him down makes her the new target. With deadly enemies closing in, Kate and James must flee together, trusting only each other as they fight to survive. In a world built on lies, faith may be the only thing that can save them. **THE SPY AND THE PREACHER—A high-stakes thriller of faith, betrayal, and the power of truth.**

One man. One mission. No time to fail.

When beloved pop star Everly Lark is kidnapped, her bodyguard, Nate Bradshaw—code name "Nighthawk"—is thrust into a relentless race against time. As he battles powerful adversaries and navigates a perilous web of danger and deception, Nate uncovers a chilling truth: Everly's captor isn't just dangerous—he's utterly obsessed. With everything on the line, Nate must outwit a cunning foe before Everly disappears forever.

THE HOWLING DAWN

A Captive's Escape.
A Pirate's Redemption.
A Love Worth Fighting For.

CHARLIE H. CAMPBELL

Scarlette Graves has spent years trapped aboard her father's pirate ship, longing for freedom from the ruthless world she was born into. Silas Hodge never expected to team up with a pirate—especially one as sharp-witted and stubborn as Scarlette. But when fate throws them together, danger closes in from all sides, forcing them to fight for survival. As past sins resurface and enemies hunt them across the sea, their only chance at freedom is to risk everything—even their hearts. **THE HOWLING DAWN is a sweeping adventure of courage, redemption, and love worth fighting for.**

Made in the USA
Monee, IL
21 March 2025

14238900R00100